Dear Parents:

Congratulations! Your child is taking the first steps on an exciting journey. The destination? Independent reading!

STEP INTO READING® will help your child get there. The program offers five steps to reading success. Each step includes fun stories and colorful art or photographs. In addition to original fiction and books with favorite characters, there are Step into Reading Non-Fiction Readers, Phonics Readers and Boxed Sets, Sticker Readers, and Comic Readers—a complete literacy program with something to interest every child.

Learning to Read, Step by Step!

Ready to Read   Preschool–Kindergarten
• big type and easy words • rhyme and rhythm • picture clues
For children who know the alphabet and are eager to begin reading.

Reading with Help   Preschool–Grade 1
• basic vocabulary • short sentences • simple stories
For children who recognize familiar words and sound out new words with help.

Reading on Your Own   Grades 1–3
• engaging characters • easy-to-follow plots • popular topics
For children who are ready to read on their own.

Reading Paragraphs   Grades 2–3
• challenging vocabulary • short paragraphs • exciting stories
For newly independent readers who read simple sentences with confidence.

Ready for Chapters   Grades 2–4
• chapters • longer paragraphs • full-color art
For children who want to take the plunge into chapter books but still like colorful pictures.

STEP INTO READING® is designed to give every child a successful reading experience. The grade levels are only guides; children will progress through the steps at their own speed, developing confidence in their reading. The F&P Text Level on the back cover serves as another tool to help you choose the right book for your child.

Remember, a lifetime love of reading starts with a single step!

For Louie —H.Z.
To Mickey, Mungo, Hugo, Louie,
Gizmo, and Hank —N.G.

Text copyright © 2015 by Harriet Ziefert
Cover art and interior illustrations copyright © 2015 by Norman Gorbaty

Visit us on the Web!
StepIntoReading.com
randomhouse.com/kids

Educators and librarians, for a variety of teaching tools, visit us at
RHTeachersLibrarians.com

Library of Congress Cataloging-in-Publication Data
Ziefert, Harriet.
Sleepy Dog, wake up! / by Harriet Ziefert ; illustrated by Norman Gorbaty.
   pages cm. — (Step into reading. Step 1)
Sequel to: Sleepy Dog.
Summary: Simple text and illustrations portray a small dog waking up, having breakfast, and getting ready to play.
ISBN 978-0-385-39106-1 (trade) — ISBN 978-0-375-97360-4 (lib. bdg.) —
ISBN 978-0-385-39107-8 (ebook)
[1. Morning—Fiction. 2. Dogs—Fiction.] I. Gorbaty, Norman, illustrator. II. Title.
PZ7.Z487Slf 2015 [E]—dc23 2014012408

Printed in the United States of America   10 9 8 7 6 5 4 3

This book has been officially leveled by using the F&P Text Level Gradient™ Leveling System.

Sleepy Dog, Wake Up!

by Harriet Ziefert

illustrated by Norman Gorbaty

Random House 🏠 New York

Chapter 1: Wake Up!

"Time to get up,
sleepyhead."
Sleepy, sleepy,
get out of bed.

Sun is up.
Cat is up.
Sleepy Dog
is NOT up!

Kiss you.

Kiss you good!

Kiss you good morning!

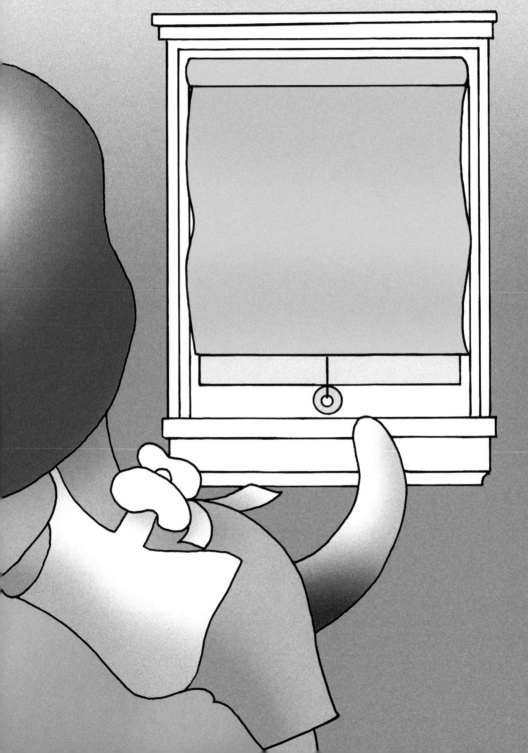

Turn off the night-light.

Turn on the day.

Open the shade.

Open the window.

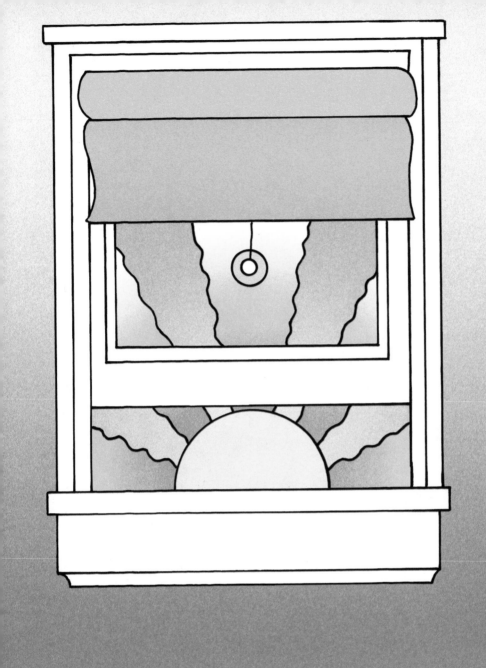

Sleepy Dog is up and
ready to start the day.

Chapter 2: Time to Eat

Sleepy Dog is eating.

Sleepy Dog is drinking milk.

Oops!

The milk spilled!

HELP!

16

17

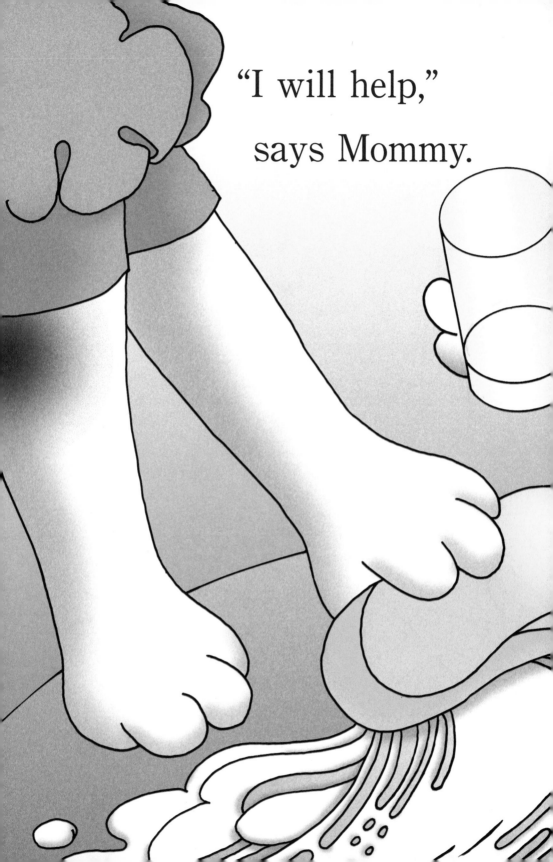

"I will help,"
says Mommy.

And so will Kitty Cat!

Happy, happy,
time to play!

Chapter 3: The Ball

Where is the ball?

Where is Sleepy Dog?
He is stuck
under the chair.

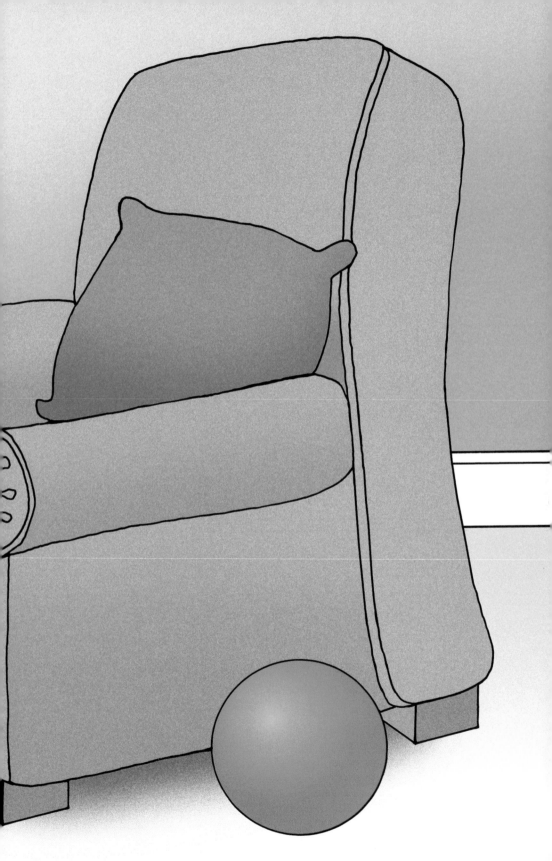

"Help!
Help me!
I am stuck!
I am stuck
under the chair!"

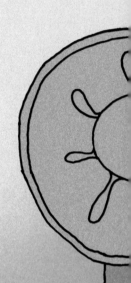

Lie down, Sleepy Dog.

Lie down flat.

Flat as a pancake.

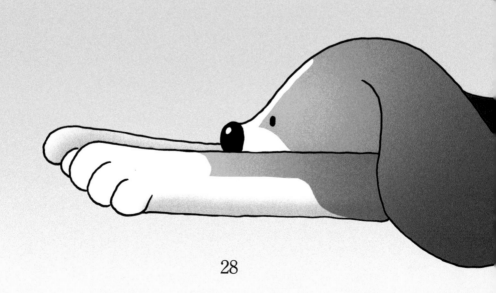

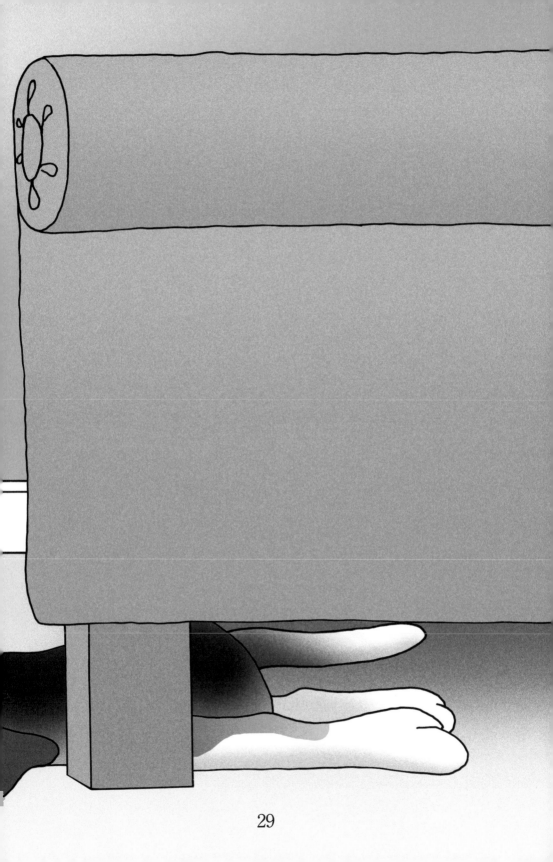

Now you are not stuck.

You are out from under!

Now it is time to play!